THE SHALOM MONITOR

ISBN 9781999031305

STORY BOOKS FOR KIDS PRESS

storybooksforkidspress@gmail.com

Formerly
Jewish Children's Book Club
105 Grove Street
Monsey NY 10952

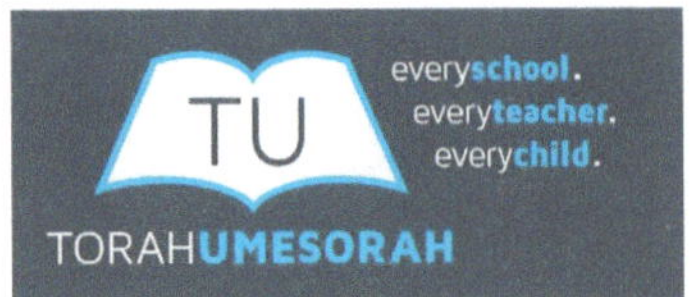

Published in conjunction with Torah Umesorah
The National Society for Hebrew Day Schools

THE SHALOM MONITOR

an "I-can-read-it-myself" book

by Aliza Cohen

Dedicated to

my grandchildren

CHAPTER 1

Yaakov was about to throw the ball to his friend Shuey when he first heard it.

"You took it!" Zev shouted.

"Did not!" Ezra yelled back.

Yaakov watched as Zev chased Ezra around the playground. What was going on?

"Hey!" Shuey said. He ran after Zev, and Yaakov followed. "Why are you fighting with Ezra?"

"He took my pet bird!" Zev shouted.

"Did not!" Ezra insisted.

"Oh yes, you did," said Zev, his eyes narrowed. He looked at Shuey. "Ezra was absent yesterday. I went to his house after school to give him his homework … and there on his porch was my pet bird. It was green with a yellow head — just like mine!"

"It's *my* bird!" Ezra shouted. "I just got it."

Yaakov looked first at Ezra, and then at Zev. Those two boys sure looked angry!

Yaakov remembered something Rebbi Pinchas had taught them. Rebbi Pinchas had explained that since the Second *Beis Hamikdash* was destroyed because of *sinas chinam*, the way to rebuild the Third *Beis Hamikdash* was through *shalom* between friends.

Yaakov had to do something to get Ezra and Zev to stop fighting! But what?

Zev started to shout some more.

"Wait!" Yaakov said. His voice squeaked, and no one even heard him.

Yaakov felt his cheeks turn hot. Of course no one was listening to him! *I am the quietest boy in the class*, he thought. *What was I thinking?*

Yaakov threw the ball at Shuey. Shuey threw it back, but Yaakov hardly saw it. He was too busy watching Zev and Ezra.

If only he could do something!

CHAPTER 2

When Yaakov came home, he ran upstairs to his room. He wanted to play with his race cars. He opened his bedroom closet, but his race cars weren't in their usual spot.

Yaakov ran to Chana's room. She was playing with his cars.

"Give me those!" he shouted. "You can't touch my things without my permission."

Chana shrugged.

"You're always touching my things!" Yaakov yelled.

Chana still didn't say a word. Yaakov scooped up his cars and put them back in his closet. Then he hung a sign on his doorknob that said "DO NOT ENTER" and shut the door.

Yaakov lay down on his bed. *Sisters*! he thought. *Chana is always taking my things. She's always giggling and getting on my nerves!*

Yaakov took out his homework from his backpack and sat at his desk. He tried to concentrate on his math questions, but he kept thinking about Zev and Ezra — and Chana. There had to be some way to make peace between Zev and Ezra. But if Chana never listened to him, how could he expect Zev and Ezra to listen?

CHAPTER 3

"Supper!" Mommy called.

Yaakov sat down at the kitchen table. What was Chana holding in her hand? Yaakov leaned over to get a better look. She had purple candies. That was Yaakov's favorite treat, but Chana never shared with him.

"Why does Chana always have so many treats?" Yaakov asked. Chana was always coming home from school with candy.

"She had a birthday party at school," Mommy explained.

Chana giggled, and Yaakov glared at her. Suddenly, he heard something chirp.

"What is that?" he asked.

The noise stopped.

"What, dear?" Mommy said.

He could hear the chirping again. "What's that noise?"

"It's my pet bird," Chana said proudly.

Yaakov stared at her. Since when did Chana have a pet bird?

Yaakov finished eating quickly. Then he got up to see the birdcage.

"Hey!" he said. "It's green with a yellow head — just like Zev's bird."

"What did you say?" Chana asked.

"Nothing," Yaakov said quickly. He watched the bird fly from one side of the cage to the other. How he wished he could take this bird and give it to Zev! That would solve his problem at school. But then he would have more problems at home with Chana.

"Where did you get this bird?" Yaakov asked.

Chana didn't answer. She lifted the birdcage.

"Careful!" Yaakov said. "Where are you taking it?"

"To my room," she said. "She's going to sleep there."

"What's her name?" Yaakov asked as he followed Chana up the stairs.

"Benjy," Chana said, and then she shut her bedroom door.

"That's a boy's name," Yaakov said.

But Chana never heard him.

Yaakov woke up the next morning, hoping that Zev and Ezra were friends again. But Zev just walked around telling anyone who would listen that Ezra had taken his bird. Yaakov scratched his forehead.

"Zev," he said. His voice squeaked, but this time Zev heard him.

"What?" Zev said. He looked upset.

Yaakov swallowed. "Remember we learned that the first principle for making *shalom* is not to hate your brother in your heart?"

"Well, wouldn't you hate someone who took something from you?" Zev said.

"Then what about the second principle?" Yaakov said. "We need to give others the benefit of the doubt. Maybe Ezra really has his own bird. How can you know for sure that he took yours?"

"I'm sure," Zev said angrily.

"Then what about the third principle?" Yaakov said. "Don't bear a grudge."

"You'd be angry too if someone took your pet," Zev said. "Besides, I miss Benjy."

Benjy? Wasn't that what Chana had called her bird?

"Wait a minute!" Yaakov said. "Zev, your bird is named Benjy?"

"Yes," Zev said. "Why?"

"I think I know where she might be," Yaakov said. So not only did Chana take his race cars without permission, she also took Zev's bird!

Zev stared at Yaakov. "Where is Benjy? Tell me!"

"I can't tell you just yet," Yaakov said. "Can you come over to my house today?"

"Why?" Zev put his hands on his hips.

"I have something to show you, but it's a surprise. I can't tell you what it is yet."

Yaakov wasn't sure how he would convince Chana to give the bird to Zev, but he knew he had to return it to its owner. Yaakov

took off his glasses and rubbed his eyes. This wasn't going to be easy, he thought.

Zev looked at him. "We should call you the Shalom Monitor," he said. "You seem to like making peace!"

Yaakov stood a little taller. Of course, he would do his best. But… would he really be able to make peace?

CHAPTER 5

Yaakov led Zev into his house. He tried to look calm, but he was worried. What if he was wrong? Or what if he was right and Chana refused to give back the bird?

"Chana!" Yaakov called as he came upstairs.

"What?" Chana poked her head out of her bedroom door.

"My friend wants to see your bird," Yaakov said.

Chana closed her bedroom door.

"Chana!" Yaakov said loudly.

She opened the door again. "What?"

"Just let us see it for a minute," he said.

"Okay," Chana said. She carefully picked up the birdcage near her bed. She brought it to the door and proudly showed it off to Zev. "Isn't she the cutest?"

"Yeah, she's pretty cute," Zev said. He looked closely at the

bird. "Can I hold the birdcage?"

"Sure," Chana said. She handed the cage to Zev.

Zev inspected the bird closely. "Benjy, is that you?"

"How did you know her name is Benjy?" Chana asked in surprise.

"Because this is my bird!" Zev said.

"No, it isn't!" Chana said. "It's *my* bird. I traded for it fair and square."

"Who gave it to you, Chana?" Yaakov asked.

"My friend Avigayil," she said.

"Avigayil? Do you mean Avigayil Silver?" Zev said. "That's my sister!"

"What did you trade for it, Chana?" Yaakov asked.

Chana looked down. "Um … your pogo stick," she finally said.

Yaakov gulped. "My pogo stick?!"

Chana nodded.

Why was she always touching his things?! How could she give away his toys?

Yaakov opened his mouth, but then he remembered how Zev had called him a Shalom Monitor. Shalom Monitors probably didn't shout. Instead, he thought about The Shalom Principles:

Step One:

Don't hate your brother (sister) in your heart.

Step two:

Give others the benefit of the doubt.

Step three:

Don't bear a grudge.

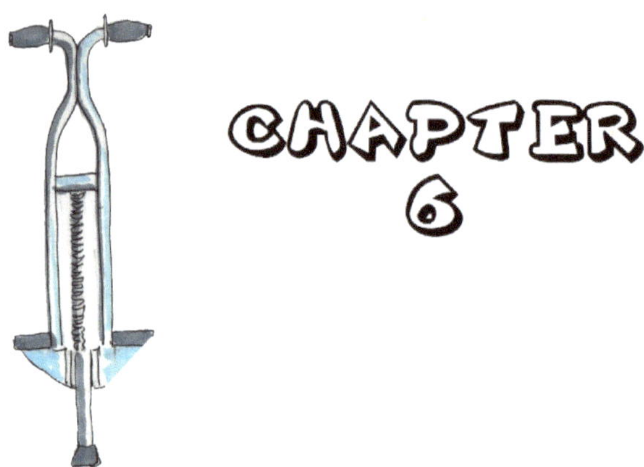

CHAPTER 6

"Chana," Yaakov said as calmly as he could, "please give Benjy back to Zev, and ask Avigayil to bring back my pogo stick."

"No!" Chana shouted. "Benjy is mine." She grabbed the birdcage from Zev's hands. The bird began to fly furiously from side to side.

"Stop that, Benjy," Chana said.

"Give it to me," Zev said. He took the birdcage back from Chana. Benjy stopped flying and looked up at Zev.

"She's mine!" Chana began to cry.

"Chana, Benjy is Zev's bird," Yaakov said. "See how she likes Zev?"

"I traded for her fair and square," Chana insisted.

"Zev, give Chana the birdcage," Yaakov said suddenly.

"Huh?" Zev was confused.

"Just let Chana hold the birdcage for a minute," Yaakov told him. He hoped his plan would work.

Zev gave the cage back to Chana. Again, the bird began to fly furiously from side to side.

"Stop that," Chana said, but Benjy continued to flap her wings.

"Now, Chana, give the bird back to Zev," Yaakov said.

"Why?" she asked, her eyes still wet with tears.

"Just do it," Yaakov told her.

She gave the cage back to Zev. The bird stopped flying and looked up at Zev.

"See, Chana? Benjy wants to be with Zev," Yaakov said. "She's not scared when she's with Zev. Look how still she is now. You want Benjy to be happy, don't you?"

"Yes," Chana whispered.

"Then what do you think you should do?" Yaakov asked gently.

"Give her back to Zev," Chana said, looking sad.

"I'm going to go home," Zev said. "I have to take care of Benjy — and I need to call Ezra to apologize."

After walking Zev downstairs, Yaakov went back into Chana's room. She was sitting on her bed.

"Chana?" Yaakov said. He

couldn't help feeling bad for her. Suddenly, she didn't seem so annoying anymore.

"What?" Chana sniffled.

"You're a real *mensch*," Yaakov said.

"Really?" she said. Her eyes brightened.

"I know it was hard for you to give up Benjy," Yaakov said. "What you did was really special."

"You think so?" Chana dried her tears with her blanket.

"Yes, I do." Yaakov gave his little sister a hug.

"I'm going to call Avigayil and tell her to bring back your pogo stick," Chana said. "I'm sorry I took it without permission."

"It's okay," Yaakov said.

Chana stood up. "You want some of my purple candies from yesterday?" she asked. "I still have some left."

"Sure," Yaakov said. "Thanks."

The two of them went downstairs together.

CHAPTER 7

The next day, Yaakov watched Zev and Ezra laughing together. He smiled — until he heard two voices shouting.

Oh no! Yaakov thought. *Shimmy and Yossi are fighting. Not again…*

Then he remembered how he had helped Zev and Ezra. He thought about how he had made peace with Chana. He felt taller than he had ever felt before.

Yaakov smiled. "The Shalom Monitor is coming to the rescue!" he said, and he ran to make peace.

Becoming
a Shalom Monitor

The Shalom Monitor can be used as a springboard to discuss the importance of making peace. Why is it important for Yaakov, the quietest boy in the class, to make peace between his classmates? Why does the argument between Zev and Ezra bother him? How is their disagreement comparable to his problems with his sister, Chana?

Although we can reinforce that the Second Beis Hamikdash was destroyed because of *sinas chinam*, baseless hatred, we can also emphasize that there is uneasiness when we are not at peace with others. In *The Shalom Monitor*, knowing **The Shalom Principles** gives Yaakov the courage to motivate others to use them as well. Instead of allowing their fights to continue, children are encouraged to find positive solutions.

The Shalom Principles:

1) Don't hate your brother (or sister) in your heart.
   Pirkei Avot 1:6

Rabbi Yisrael Salanter stated that all Jews are one body. We should view the entire Jewish nation as *"acheinu kol beis Yisrael"* — our brothers.

Ask your child:

How do you feel when someone slights you?

How do you react in response?

How can you express your feelings without hurting the other person?

2) Give others the benefit of the doubt. *Vayikra 19:17*

How can we judge others favorably?

Did you ever give someone the benefit of the doubt?

3) **Don't bear a grudge.** *Vayikra 19:18*

How do you feel toward someone who has wronged you?

What can you do instead of bearing a grudge against someone who has hurt you?

By teaching children to live a life of peace, we are teaching them how to separate the person from the behavior. The first principle shows children that they can dislike what someone did and be upset about their choices, but they cannot hate them for it. The second principle encourages children to ask: Do I have proof for my claim? And even if the claim is true, the third principle mandates not to bear a grudge. Your friend might have done something wrong, but it's up to you to choose the correct response.

With these three principles in place, may our homes and lives become peaceful and pleasant — as befitting the Jewish nation.

Shalom!